AF559681

The Monkey's Revenge

The Monkey's Revenge

TWO STORIES FROM THE PANCHATANTRA

Retold by

MEENA ARORA NAYAK

Illustrations by

Ajanta Guhathakurta

ALEPH

ALEPH BOOK COMPANY
An independent publishing firm
promoted by ***Rupa Publications India***

First published in India in 2024
by Aleph Book Company
7/16 Ansari Road, Daryaganj
New Delhi 110 002

ISBN: 978-81-974969-9-8

1 3 5 7 9 10 8 6 4 2

Printed in India

The Tale of How the King's Rash Decision Led to the Monkey's Revenge

A city was ruled by a king by the name of Chandra. He had many sons, and they loved monkeys. They would play with the animals all day long and feed them all kinds of delicious foods and mithai.

The chief of that troop of monkeys was very learned and well versed in all niti

ideals expounded in law books such as *Shukra Niti*, *Brihaspati Niti*, and *Chanakya Niti*. He also lived his life according to these ideals and taught his monkeys the same.

In the king's palace was a flock of sheep who were also the princes' playmates. The boys would climb on their backs and ride around, as they ran here and there, bleating. One of the sheep had developed the habit of sneaking into the kitchen to eat whatever it could find, and every time it did that, the servants would chase it out, trying to hit it with whatever they could lay their hands on—pots and pans made of copper, bronze, wood, or clay.

The chief of the monkeys watched this tableau play out every morning—the sheep entering the kitchen, foraging for food, and the kitchen staff chasing him out. He had a feeling that this daily contention would end up hurting the monkeys. He reasoned: this sheep

has acquired the taste of grain, and the people who work in the kitchen are getting angrier by the day, chasing him out with whatever they can lay their hands on. Right now, they're grabbing pots and pans to hit him. Tomorrow, they may even grab a burning log of

wood from the stove. If they touch that sheep with it, he'll instantly catch fire, because he hasn't been shorn, and his wool is long and combustible. The sheep will then run out, bleating in pain, and make for the stable to roll in the hay. But the hay in the stable is dry, and it'll burst into flames, instantly. Soon, the whole stable will be aflame, and the king's best horses will get burned. The divine physician of horses, Shalihotra, has said that fat from a monkey's body is the best salve to alleviate the pain of a horse's burn wounds. Therefore, I foresee us monkeys meeting a quick demise, if such an eventuality occurs.

Thus, the monkey chief called his

troop and apprised them of what was happening in the kitchen every day and how it could imperil them. He said to them,

> The house with needless conflict
> is not a suitable place to live.
> Anyone who values his life
> should leave it as soon as
> possible,

Also,

> Strife destroys homes.
> Bitter words destroy friendships.
> A cruel king destroys the
> kingdom.
> Bad action destroys a good name.

'So, my friends, we should leave this place and go to the forest before we are killed because of some silly conflict between the kitchen staff and that food-loving sheep.'

Some of the younger monkeys laughed at the old chief's warning. 'It appears that old age has affected your intelligence,' they said to him. 'It is said,

> The mouths of infants and aged
> are toothless and drooling,
> So also is their intelligence.

Are you telling us to leave the luxuries of the palace and all the delicious mithai that the princes feed us and go off into the forest, where we'll have to eat tart, bitter, and dried up fruits from the trees? How can we do that?'

The old monkey's eyes filled with tears. 'You young fools, you don't know,

> Luxuries can yield results
> as harmful as poison,
> just like a kuchla fruit is
> sweet but deadening.

Obviously, you don't want to heed my warning. But I can't stay here and see the destruction of my clan with my own eyes; therefore, I'm leaving for the forest. It is said,

> Those people are blessed who
> don't have to see

friends in adversity, enemies
ruling their land,
their clan's ruin, and dissolution
of their country.'

Hence, the old monkey chief left for the forest, and the very next morning, what he had foreseen happened: the sheep got into the kitchen, and the cook, not finding anything else within reach, took a burning log and hit him with it. The sheep's wool immediately caught fire, and he ran out, bleating in pain, heading straight for the hay in the stable. The dry hay lit into a blaze, and the whole stable was engulfed in flames. Many of the horses burned to death, others became blinded, and still others broke their tethers and began to run helter-skelter, squealing and neighing.

The men who took care of the stable were thrown into confusion, not knowing whether to put out the fire or to rescue the horses. When the king got news of the injuries his royal horses had received in the fire, he immediately called the veterinarians and commanded them to prepare an ointment to relieve their pain. The physicians consulted their books and said to the king, 'Maharaj, Lord Shalihotraji himself has said,

> Monkeys' fat can alleviate
> the pain

> of horses suffering from burns,
> as quickly as the sun dispels
> darkness.

Hence, you should acquire monkeys' fat as soon as you can, or the horses will expire from their burns.'

Consequently, the king ordered all the monkeys in the kingdom to be put to death.

When that old monkey chief heard about his sons, nephews, brothers, and friends being slaughtered, he was deeply grieved. For days, he wandered in the forest, despondent, not eating or drinking. Then he began to think about revenge.

It is said,

> Be it through greed or fear,
> but those who can bear to
> see their clan being harmed
> by enemies are detestable and
> dastardly.

One day, that old monkey, looking for water to quench his thirst came upon a lake adorned with lotuses. Approaching it, he carefully looked around and noticed that while there were plenty of footprints, of both animals and people going to the lake, there were none returning. Thus, he knew that this lake was inhabited by a crocodile or some other feral creature, who dragged anyone that touched the water into the lake. Therefore, to avoid direct contact with the water, the monkey broke off a lotus stalk and, dipping it in the lake, sucked the water through it.

As he took a long draught of cool water, a ferocious rakshasa, wearing a brilliant necklace of jewels, rose out of the lake.

'O monkey,' the rakshasa thundered. 'This is my lake. Anyone who immerses even a toe into it becomes my food. I eat him up. But you are more intelligent than anyone I have seen. I'm very impressed by the way you are drinking without letting even a tip of your toe touch the water. I'm very pleased with your

intelligent mind. Ask me for a boon—anything you desire.'

'How much can you eat?' the monkey asked the rakshasa.

'If a hundred, or a thousand, or ten thousand, or even a lakh creatures come into my lake, I can devour all of them. But outside this lake, even a tiny fox can scare me. I have no power outside the water.'

'I have a great enemy—a king. If you can lend me your jewelled necklace, I can entice him to come here to this lake, along with his family.'

The rakshasa did not even pause to think. Removing his necklace, he handed it to the monkey. 'Friend, here it is. Go and do what you have to.'

The monkey put the necklace around his neck and went to pay a visit to the king's neighbourhood. There, swinging from tree to tree, walking in plain sight on the roofs of buildings, he made sure he was seen by several people. They asked him, 'O monkey chief, where have you been all these days? And where did you get such a beautiful necklace that outshines even the sun?'

'In the forest, in a certain spot, there is a big lake that Lord Kubera has built. Whoever bathes in that lake on Ravivaar (Sunday) at exactly the time when the sun is half risen, he will emerge from the lake with just such a necklace around his neck.'

As the monkey had hoped, his words soon reached the king, and he ordered his men to bring the monkey to him. 'O chief of monkeys, is there really such a lake in the forest where you can receive such a jewelled necklace simply by bathing in it?' he asked. 'Is this true?'

'Maharaj, see this necklace around my neck. Is this not proof of what I say? If you, too, desire such a necklace, then send someone with me, and I'll show him where the lake is.'

'If that is the case, I, myself, will come with you, along with all my servants and my family, and all of us will take a dip. That way each of us can receive such a necklace.'

On the night before Ravivaar, the king ordered his carriages and, carrying the monkey on his lap, he rode with his whole family and entourage of servants to the lake, and arrived there just before daybreak.

Someone has rightly said,

She who subjugates even the
richest,
Making them wander from place
to place
And do evil acts of injustice
grave—
Propitiations to that Devi of
Craving.

He who has a hundred, craves a thousand.
He who has a thousand, craves a lakh.
An owner of a lakh, craves a kingdom.
And one who rules a kingdom, craves for gold.
All are enslaved by craving; no one is content.

In old age, hair turns grey,
teeth and nails fall out,
ears, eyes, all other senses dull.
But craving remains forever youthful.

As the sun began to peek over the horizon, the monkey reminded the king, 'To achieve the boon of the necklace, you have to take a dip in the lake at exactly the time when the sun is half risen. Therefore, please advise your men and family members to jump in exactly at that time. I, myself, will wait here with you and, after that, I'll take you to a special spot in the lake where there are numerous such jewelled necklaces.'

At the king's order at mid-sunrise, everyone jumped into the lake. And, as soon as they did, the rakshasa, who was underwater, devoured them. The king watched the water for a long time, waiting for them to emerge, and when

not a single one reappeared, he turned to the monkey and asked him, 'Why isn't anyone coming out? Why is it taking them so long?'

The monkey didn't respond. Instead, he leapt on a tree and climbed to a high branch, and from there he spoke: 'O evil king, your relatives and attendants have all been eaten by the rakshasa who lives in the lake. I have taken my revenge. Just be thankful that I spared you. It is said,

> Do to others what they do
> to you.
> Harm him who harms you.
> Be cruel to him who is cruel
> to you.

You will not be faulted for this.

You killed my clan, O king, and I have killed yours.'

People say that the king was so devastated that he refused to ride back to the palace in his carriage and walked all the way. After he left, the rakshasa emerged from the water and said to the monkey, 'By drinking water with a lotus stalk you not only managed to get your revenge, but you also won my friendship. And you brought the jewelled necklace back intact as well. Your intelligence is truly applaudable.'

The Tale of the Iron-eating Mice and the Boy-devouring Falcon

In a town lived a businessman, named Jirnadhana (depleted wealth). Over the years, he suffered several business losses, and his money depleted, till his situation became dire. Hence, he decided to go to a foreign land and try his luck there. He thought,

In a place where a person has
enjoyed
the rich rewards of his labour
and effort,
how can he then live a respectful
life,
when his money begins to diminish?

He also felt dejected because,

When a man lives in a town for
many years
with head held high in pride
and esteem,
he loses all respect of people
he knows,
if his status becomes meagre
and pitiful.

‘It is best for me to leave town and try to rebuild my wealth in another town,’ he said to himself and, packing up everything, vacated his house. However, he had in his house a heavy iron scale, weighing about one thousand palas, that he had inherited from his ancestors, and he didn’t want to sell it or give it away. Therefore, before leaving town, he went to a fellow businessman and acquaintance and requested him to keep his scale safe, promising him that he would come to get it when he returned.

Jirnadhana spent many years abroad, and when he returned, he went directly to his businessman friend’s house to retrieve his scale. However, when he asked him

for it, the response he got was: 'Dear man, we have searched everywhere for your scale, but it is nowhere to be found. It appears that mice may have eaten it.'

Jirnadhana was shocked to hear this, but he quickly concealed his reaction and said to the businessman, 'Sethji, if my iron scale was eaten by mice, then it is not your fault, because this is how the world is. Nothing lasts forever. Everyone and everything are transient and must leave this earth. If the scale has left, then what is the surprise in that? Be it so. But I have a small favour to ask. I've just returned from overseas, and I need to go and bathe at the river. I request you to please send your youngest son with me with a change of clothes, soap, oil, towel, etc.'

The businessman was a little taken aback by the request, but he figured that, after robbing the man of his scale, he owed him at least that much. So, calling his little boy, Dhanadeva (lord of wealth), he instructed him: 'Boy, this is your uncle. He needs to go to the river for a bath. Go with him and take the items he requests; then stay there till he brings you back home.'

Oh! Someone has rightly said,
True devotion or respect is never
the cause
for why someone would do
another's work.

It is fear or greed, or some such thing
that propels people to help others.
Proof of this can be found in flattery;
no one flatters another out of devotion.

When one receives utmost
deference without cause,
one should look at it with suspicion.
It disguises deceits and treacheries,
which will be revealed at the end.

The little boy gathered the items and

accompanied Jirnadhana to the river. Telling him to sit by his clothes, Jirnadhana took a long bath, and, thereafter, taking the boy by the hand, he led him to a cave in the mountain. 'Stay here, son,' he said, gently. 'Don't be afraid. I'll return shortly.' Then he covered the mouth of the cave with a rock and went to see the businessman.

Seeing him return alone, the businessman asked, 'Where is my son? I sent him with you to the river. Why hasn't he returned with you?'

'Sethji,' said Jirnadhana, 'as the boy was sitting on the bank, a falcon swooped down and grabbed him and flew away.'

'What?' said the shocked businessman. 'You liar. What are you saying? How can a falcon carry away a boy?'

'O truthful seth, just as a falcon can't carry away a boy, mice can't eat a massive iron scale. If you want your son back, return my scale,' said Jirnadhana.

The two businessmen then began hurling insults at each other, and their quarrel escalated to such an extent that they ended up in the king's court.

'I'm devastated, Maharaj,' said the father of the boy. 'This wicked man has kidnapped my son. Please order him to return my child. How can such a heinous act be allowed in your reign?'

The magistrate turned to Jirnadhana

and asked him, 'Where is the boy, and why did you kidnap him?'

'Maharaj, I did not kidnap him. As the boy was sitting on the bank, a falcon suddenly swooped down and grabbed him. I saw it with my own eyes, but there was nothing I could do. It happened so suddenly.'

'What you are saying is obviously not true,' the magistrate said sternly. 'How can a falcon carry away a boy?'

'Maharaj, in a place where an iron scale, weighing thousands of palas can be eaten by mice, there, a falcon can certainly carry away a boy. Believe me. There is no doubt about it.'

'Explain yourself,' the magistrate told

Jirnadhana, and he related the whole tale from beginning to end.

Hearing the story, everyone in the court began to laugh. The magistrate then ordered the businessman to return Jirnadhana's scale and for Jirnadhana to return the boy.